# The Tiptoe Guide
## to Tracking Mermaids

by Ammi-Joan Paquette          Illustrated by Marie Letourneau

Tanglewood • Terre Haute. IN

Published by Tanglewood Publishing, Inc., April 2012

Design by Amy Alick Perich

Tanglewood Publishing, Inc.
4400 Hulman Street
Terre Haute, IN 47803
www.tanglewoodbooks.com

Printed in the USA
10 9 8 7 6 5 4 3 2 1

ISBN 1-933718-59-5
      978-1-933718-59-0

*Library of Congress Cataloging-in-Publication Data*

Paquette, Ammi-Joan.
 The tiptoe guide to tracking mermaids / by Ammi-Joan Paquette ; illustrated by Marie Letourneau.
    p. cm.
 Summary: While following instructions for spotting mermaids, the reader is introduced to a variety of marine life found along the seashore.
 ISBN-13: 978-1-933718-59-0
 ISBN-10: 1-933718-59-5
 [1. Marine animals--Fiction. 2. Seashore--Fiction. 3. Mermaids--Fiction.] I. Le Tourneau, Marie, ill. II. Title.
 PZ7.P2119Tg 2012
 [E]--dc23
                        2011040976

For Peggy, who believed.
-AP

To beachcombers everywhere:
I hope you find your mermaid.
-ML

On hot summer days, the beaches are packed with people swimming, splashing, or lying in the sun. But there are other days—magical ones—when the beach is empty.

Whoosh! The wind tosses up the sand in curling eddies. Kazoom! The waves cymbal-crash against the shore. *Yes!*

Days like these are just right for tracking mermaids.

This quiet seashore is the perfect place to start. We've found a perfect pink conch shell. Listen carefully. . . . Does it have any secrets to tell us?

Mermaids live out in the ocean, but they like to come ashore to play. There are no mermaids here today. But . . . we can leave them a surprise for when they come back!

Where to next? Oh! Just ahead . . . where the rocks jut out into the sea like a long, craggy finger.

This tide pool is just the kind of place where baby mermaids love to splash on a hot day. I wonder if they ever come here?

Is this a treasure box?
Or a mermaid's secret
collection of jewels?

With an abalone shell mirror and a cowrie comb, a mermaid can primp and style herself so she is ready for any occasion.

This shell has a tiny hole at the top. With the fine strand of a spider's web, a mermaid can string herself a necklace that will glow like sunset.

This sand dollar is smooth and shiny. Let's see how many more we can collect. Maybe this will tempt the mermaids out of hiding.

I wonder what treasures
the sand dollars might buy
at the market?

Mermaids love to eat. Some of their favorite treats grow along the seashore: tender sea lettuce and sugar kelp. We'll leave a handful of Queen Anne's lace petals for them to sprinkle on top as a garnish.

Look at all these friendly crabs skittering around! They must be the clean-up crew. They seem to enjoy munching on the mermaids' leftovers. Mmmm!

When mealtime is over, mermaids like to take a relaxing underwater nap. In a hammock of woven weeds, they curl up and sleep for hours. Tiny minnows play peek-a-boo in their long hair, and nibble every last bit of algae from their glittering scales.

Those mermaids sleep the afternoon away, waiting until the cool of evening before popping up for some more dolphin-chasing, wave-hopping, water-splashing fun. Can you see any mermaids anywhere?

We look high. We look low.
Where could those mermaids
be hiding?

What else do mermaids love?
Hide-and-seek in the coral reefs.
Tag with their seahorse
buddies. Undersea acrobatics
to the thrumming beat of the
ocean surf.

Mermaids do love all of these
things, but our day is nearly over
and we have not found a single
one. We can't—we shouldn't—
we *won't* give up!

And . . . wait! What is that all the
way over there? Is that something
glistening?

It's a bottle—with a
message inside. The
cork slides out: Pop!
A sheet of paper
shimmies into our
hands: Bloop!
And . . . **Swish!** here
is a message for us
all to read.

Listen to the Secrets of the Conch Shell

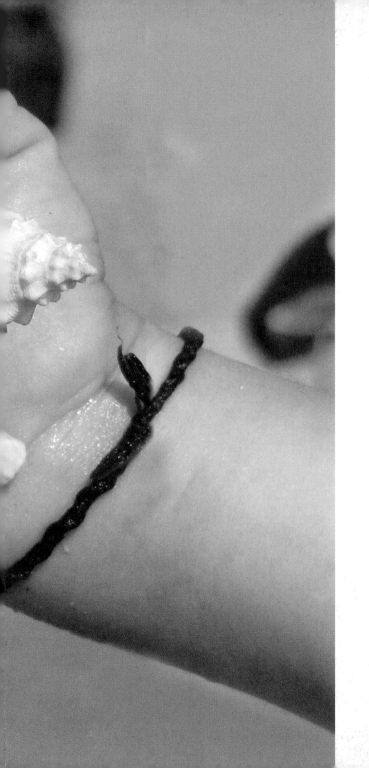

Where did that shell go?
Here it is!
We're listening.
Can you hear anything?

Yes! It sounds like . . . mermaids!
They are telling us where to go.

Around one rock.
Over two.
Up and down again.
And then . . .

MAGIC!